STOP

SENDING MISSIONARIES!

SIX REASONS WE SHOULD
STOP SENDING MISSIONARIES
AND WHY THEY ARE ALL WRONG.

RICHARD MALM

Richard Malm
www.rickmalm.com

More Resources:
For more resources from the author, including videos, podcasts and material for use in small groups, go to www.RickMalm.com

STOP Sending Missionaries/Richard Malm. —1st ed.

ISBN 978-0-9985085-7-3

TABLE OF CONTENTS

GOD HAS A SOFT SPOT IN HIS HEART
FOR SIMPLE PEOPLE
WHO WILL SIMPLY OBEY HIM -
EVEN IF RELUCTANTLY.

Dedication

To the tens of thousands of flawed, unqualified, inadequate ordinary people who, throughout the ages, responded to an invitation from their Lord to follow Him into the unknown.

You went in spite of doubts, questions, fears and insecurity...... and God smiled.

INTRODUCTION

WHY
"Stop Sending Missionaries!"

You can tell a lot about a person by listening to their prayer requests. One woman tearfully requested prayer for her friend who was in a coma. As she passionately shared her concern it soon became evident the "friend" she was talking about was a character in her favorite soap opera! Yes, you can tell what's close to a person's heart by what they ask prayer for.

I recently saw a surprising prayer request. What they were asking prayer for wasn't surprising. What made it unusual was the person who was submitting the request.

It was Jesus Himself! And His request tells us a lot about what is important to Him, what is close to His heart.

The Prayer Request of Jesus

What was His concern? What was the topic close to His heart? What did He ask us to pray for? He saw a white harvest – millions waiting to hear about Him – but not enough workers in the harvest field. So, He asked us to pray for more workers.

> *Pray to the Lord who is in charge of the harvest;*
> *ask him to send more workers into his fields.*
> **- Matthew 9:38 NLT**

Jesus sees a problem. He says the answer to the problem is not more Bible colleges, seminaries, theologians or even more churches. Of course, none of these are bad, but His solution is more laborers – common, ordinary folks who are willing to get in there, get their hands dirty and work.

In a previous book, *"Commission To Every Nation, How People Just Like You Are Blessing the Nations,"* I tell how God used a very unlikely candidate for ministry to establish a missionary sending agency that has enabled thousands to follow their dream into the mission field. That "very unlikely candidate for ministry" was me.

That book contains an addendum that answers four questions people frequently ask about the validity of missions in our globally connected, pluralistic 21st century world.

The responses to that addendum convinced me that the answers to those questions needed more exposure than just as an afterword. I heard from Christians who attend missional, Bible teaching churches that confessed they had been guilty of asking those very questions: 'Why worry about foreign missions when we have so many in need right here at home? Why not just support national workers who can do the job cheaper? And other "why send missionaries" questions.

It seems that no matter how regularly mission and church leaders talk about the importance of world evangelization – and I am concerned that it is becoming a rare and infrequent topic of public preaching and teaching – many Christians still have questions as to why we should expend so much energy and money on people that we will likely never see or meet. The Lord asks, "Who will go?" while we are asking, "Why go?" (Isaiah 6:8)

Since 1990 I have served as a missionary and, as the founder / president of Commission To Every Nation and Commission Ministers Network - two organizations that help people follow the call of God into missions and other ministry opportunities - I have had the privilege of meeting literally thousands of missionaries and ministers from the US, Canada and many other nations. And, though I have never met two who are exactly alike, I have found nearly all of them, no matter their country of citizenship, have one thing in common.

Most of them have family and friends who do not understand their calling. They have faced many questions about the need and validity of what they're doing. Well-meaning family and friends have often presented challenging questions that are hard to answer.

Most missionaries don't have all the answers as to **why** they are going. They just sense a call, an invitation from heaven, perhaps even a compelling command, to go. And they are driven to obey that call and sacred invitation.

I present this little book as a tool to encourage them and also as a resource they can hand to those who are sincerely concerned about their well-being and have genuine questions about the need for sending missionaries.

I pray this book will:

- Reignite the heart of any who have wanted to go but who have been dissuaded from following that desire.

- Calm the soul of those who are understandably concerned about loved ones who are making life altering decisions to follow what they sense God calling them to do.

- Answer questions for those who have sincerely wondered if it was time to **STOP Sending Missionaries.**

Ite inflammate omnia;

Rick

Until our hearts
are fully captured
by that which
captivates His heart,
our pulse will never
beat fully in sync
with His.

His heart beats
for the lost,
for the nations.

- RM
Psalm 2:8

CHAPTER 1

STOP
"Sending Missionaries!"

There are plenty of needs here at home.

Occasionally, well-meaning people sincerely ask me why we should send missionaries to other countries when there are so many lost and so many needs in our own neighborhoods. I usually give a one-word answer – access.

Access

Sadly, it's true there are millions of unbelievers in the United States and Canada, but there are also millions of believers in the US and Canada who can easily tell them about the Lord. Furthermore, a person in North America can hear the news of Jesus through 24/7/365 Christian radio, television, and online, all in a host of languages. We have access to Christian bookstores, magazines, free Bibles in hotel rooms, on our phones, and churches on nearly every corner. A seeker in the US or Canada can find the Truth.

But there are millions of people in the world who would be clueless if you asked them about Jesus. They would have no idea who He was, what He did or, in some cases, even what a "Jesus" is. One pioneer Indian missionary venturing into an unreached area told this story. As he walked into the village, he approached the first person he saw and began to talk about the Lord. When he mentioned the name "Jesus," the listener suddenly seemed to understand and directed him to a small building at the end of the dusty street. Inside he found a man who repaired sewing machines. Having no idea what a "Jesus" was, the helpful villager assumed it was a brand of sewing machine and this newcomer in the village had a broken "Jesus" that needed repair.

The people in this area not only had never heard of Jesus, but if this missionary had not gone they would have had no way to hear. A first century missionary summed it up this way, "Everyone who calls on the name of the LORD will be saved. But how can they call on him to save them unless they believe in him? And how can they believe in him if they have never heard about him? And how can they hear about him unless someone tells them?" (Romans 10:13, 14 NLT)

It is estimated that in some areas of the world, there is only one Christian worker of any kind (a pastor, lay leader, missionary, etc.) for every one million people. These people have no way to hear the gospel unless someone from outside their world goes to them with the message.

To paraphrase Oswald Smith, the founder of The People's Church in Toronto, Canada, "How can we justify allowing someone to hear and reject the gospel multiple times when there are so many who have never had the opportunity to hear it even once?"

We Don't Have To Choose

And here is the best news. While it's true that we have many lost friends in our own neighborhoods and we need to reach them, we don't have to stop supporting and sending cross-cultural missionaries to do that. It doesn't cost a dime for Christians in North America to reach their neighbors. We can, and must, reach both those across the street and those across the globe.

God has given us all the resources we need. We simply need to mobilize the church to be the church and reach our neighbors while still sending missionaries to our global neighbors. There's no reason to consider this an either/or decision.

Who is my neighbor?

When Jesus was asked, "Who is my neighbor?" he told a story we call "The Good Samaritan." (Luke 10) It is about a man, a (despised by the Jews) Samaritan, who expressed compassion to a stranger. We always assume the beaten man was a Jew because he started his journey in Jerusalem but, curiously, we are never actually told his nationality. Furthermore, he was stripped of his clothing so the Samaritan had no way of knowing this man's nationality or socio-economic status. He was just a fellow human being in need of care and compassion.

Jesus then asked, "Who was the neighbor to the man who fell among thieves?" The obvious answer, "The man who had compassion." This Samaritan, made himself a neighbor by having compassion, showing mercy, by sacrificing and taking the risk of being kind to another human being without regard to his race, culture or religion.

Jesus then said, "Go and do the same thing." Go show compassion. Go treat every person as your neighbor. Go help those in need with the resources you have received. Go and make the whole world, every desperate soul you encounter, your neighbor.

John Wesley claimed, "The world is my parish." Based upon this parable, "The world is also my neighbor." It's my responsibility, in response to the command of Jesus, to love every fellow traveler on this human journey as I love myself. I am to show compassion to all in need, not just those who live within the national boundaries I find drawn on a map. When Jesus looks at us, He does not see skin color. When He looks at our world, He doesn't see the colors of countries, continents and national boundary lines that we use to divide us. He only sees the color of our hearts.

To obey the command to love our neighbor we must realize our "neighbor" is not just those who live in our city, state or nation. We are commanded to see every human being, every wounded fellow traveler, every person in need, as our neighbor and reach out to them with the same love that caused Jesus to reach out, leave heaven and come to us.

Obedience

Jesus told us to go locally and to the ends of the earth. (Acts 1:8) He did not give us the liberty to pick one or the other. That should be all the reason we need to support missions "in Jerusalem, and in all Judea, and in Samaria **and** unto the uttermost part of the earth."

If the apostles had waited until all Jerusalem and Judea and Samaria had heard the gospel before they reached out to the ends of the earth, it's quite possible that today neither you nor I would have had the opportunity to know Jesus.

When Jesus looks at our world, He doesn't see the colors of countries, continents and national boundary lines that we use to divide us. He only sees the color of our hearts.

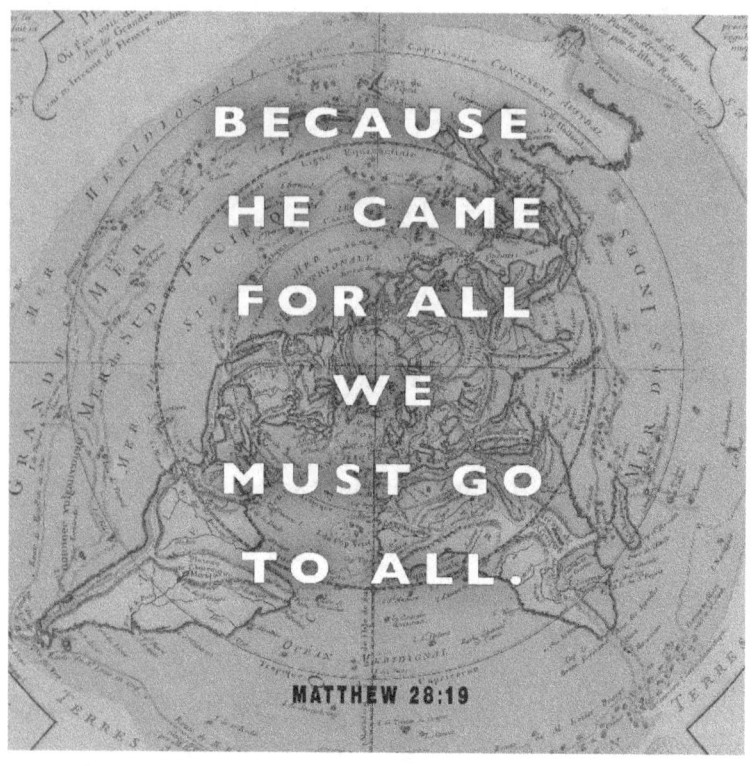

'Everyone who calls on the name of the Lord will be saved.' How, then, can they call on the one they have not believed in? And how can they believe in the one of whom they have not heard? And how can they hear without someone preaching to them? And how can anyone preach unless they are sent?

- Romans 10:13-15

CHAPTER 2

STOP
"Sending Missionaries!"

National workers can do it cheaper.

Tomas is a respected leader among his Mayan people, a former mayor and now converted Christian. His people trust him. He understands the culture and speaks several Mayan languages as well as Spanish. Though he stands barely over 5 feet tall he is a spiritual giant. He fearlessly and repeatedly risked his life pastoring God's people during the brutal civil war that devastated his land. He and his family live simply, and for just a few dollars a month we can send him to minister full time to his Ixil people in the mountains of Northern Guatemala.

Examples like this lead some to ask, "Why send North American missionaries when the nationals can do it?" It's a logical question, especially when the resources available for missions seem so limited, and the need so unlimited. It's cheaper. They already speak the language. There are no cultural barriers. They cannot be deported if the political tide turns against Christian missionaries. Perhaps the day of sending North American missionaries is over, and we should just support national workers.

I Support Supporting Nationals

I believe in helping men such as my friend, Tomas, but I'm also concerned that a narrow "either/or attitude" is more of a plot than a plan–a plot to undermine and slow the work of world evangelism. Our options are not, "either support nationals or send missionaries." The task is so big we must do both. Here are six reasons why we cannot just support national workers in hopes that they will accomplish the Great Commission given by Jesus to the entire church.

1. Is It Cheaper?

Often, but not always, it is cheaper to support national workers. They require less preparation because it is their own language and culture and they usually can live more simply in their home country. Let's face it, Christians love bargains. Sending money instead of sending people is absolutely easier. It requires little sacrifice. And, perhaps most importantly, it does not mess with my comfort zone.

Like a country that hires mercenaries to battle for them, we can stay home, enjoy our comfy couches and other luxuries of life, while paying others to shed the tears and spill their sweat and blood. I will send $20 or $200 or $2000. I will send whatever it costs, as long as I don't have to send my own sons and daughters, my own flesh and blood – as long as I don't have to sacrifice self or my lifestyle.

But God Himself set the example. The Greatest Missionary of all, Jesus, left the comforts of Heaven to come to us, to walk among the filth and mire of humanity. He sent prophets (national workers), even angels to speak for Him. But, ultimately, He had to come himself, in flesh, to fully reveal the message of God's tender mercy. We dare not simply send others. Because He came for all, we must go to all.

2. Cheaper Is Not Always Better

"If it sounds too good to be true, it probably is."

"You get what you pay for."

These maxims are often as true in missions as they are in other areas of life. Cheaper does not always mean better. Just being from a country does not automatically mean you have the skills, calling or heart necessary for effective ministry in that country. I'll bet you can name at least 5 people – North Americans - that are impressive on the surface, know the language and know the culture, but that you would not want to represent you, or the Lord, in your own country. Just being from a country does not automatically make you a capable, called or effective minister.

Like North American ministers, there are some effective and there are some not-so-effective national workers. And, unfortunately, often the most visible, the most vocal, the ones that grab the attention of visiting outsiders are the head and shoulders taller "Sauls" while the hard-working "Davids" are never seen because they are out in the field diligently caring for sheep. It's nearly impossible to tell the treacherous Sauls from the faithful Davids if you do not have culturally astute people on the ground for a long period of time to observe the national ministers in action, observe the response of the local people to their lives and measure the fruit and effectiveness of their ministry.

It's easy to create reports, videos, and even onsite visits that make "not-so-effective" appear awesome. Stories abound of ineffective national workers (and missionaries) who simply took advantage of their North American donors' generosity and naiveté. It is impossible to accurately evaluate what is really happening from a long distance "snap-shot" perspective rather than a close-up movie view. Cheaper *is* cheaper – but not necessarily better or even as good as.

3. The Need Is So Great

I was working with a missionary in Oaxaca, Mexico to build bridges into an unreached village. Are you as surprised as I was when I learned there are thousands of villages in Mexico, our southern neighbor, that have not been reached with the gospel and, that you risk your life to enter many of these villages to present the message?

We were going door to door handing out gift bags of toiletry items – a rare treat for many in this village. While taking a break from the hot sun, a young local man timidly approached us and cautiously shared his story. Looking to make sure no one could hear, he explained that he was a Christian – to his knowledge, the only one in his village. He had worked a few years in the US where a Christian employer introduced him to the message of salvation.

He expressed how grateful he was we had come because he had wanted to share what had happened to him but was afraid of being ostracized and possibly even beaten for abandoning their traditional religion. Plus, his understanding of the faith was so basic he felt he couldn't accurately explain what had happened to him in a way that would help others come to believe as well.

We encouraged him and, amazingly, later that day we encountered another young man with a similar story. We were able to introduce them to one another and later I was told they were able to plant a seedling of a church in that community.

That village is a microcosm of many areas, even some nations, in our world. In some places there are not enough national workers to accomplish the task without outside help. In other places the Christians have only a basic level of understanding of the faith and feel unable to explain how the death of a man 2000 years ago impacts their daily lives today.

Imagine a country where there are only five Christians for every 100,000 people—and those five might live scattered across the map. Without outside reinforcements, a handful of believers can't reach their nation regardless of the amount of financial resources we pump into their coffers.

4. God Has Given A Powerful Platform

Foreigners often have a "platform" that locals do not. When I first moved to Central America my Spanish teacher, who happened to be a believer, stopped in the middle of a class one day, looked at me and asked, "Why do people listen more to you?"

I had no idea what he was asking and thought, perhaps, my weak Spanish was the problem. Then he went on to explain how he had repeatedly shared the gospel with people he knew, and they would not listen. Then a "gringo" with horrid Spanish would stumble through a gospel presentation and his friends would accept Jesus.

A Kachiquel Mayan man told how he came to the Lord because a group of white people visited his remote village. "Even as a boy I thought, 'Why would these rich, white people come to my poor village? What they have must be very important for them to come all this way to give it us.'" He listened and believed.

As North Americans, we're going to give account for how we use this platform the Lord has given us. Hollywood, Nashville and Madison Avenue marketers have taken advantage of it to spread American movies, music, materialism and debauchery around the world. Surely the message of the church needs to be proclaimed as loudly from this platform of privilege while it still exists in at least some countries.

5. People Are People

Imagine you teach Sunday School and discover that 5 other teachers get paid $400 a week for teaching. You get paid nothing and, in fact, have to spend your own money to buy crayons for the kids in your class. Would you have a problem with that? Most of us would begin to wonder, "Am I not good enough," or "Maybe I'm not really wanted," or "This isn't fair," or even "Why should

I continue to sacrifice when I'm not appreciated or wanted anyway?"

In the same way, an influx of foreign money to support some national workers can create jealousy and undermine volunteerism in the local church. It can imply that you should be paid (and paid well) to do ministry.

I know what you're thinking and you're right. Christians shouldn't feel this way. But they do. In fact, I have to admit I probably would, too. People are people, no matter what country they're from. Tossing money into a situation can complicate and cloud relationships as well as create suspicion and jealousy – even among good people who love Jesus.

As I said earlier, I'm all in favor of supporting national workers but if not done wisely our well-intentioned efforts can often add confusion, hurt feelings and division.

6. His Ways Are Not Our Ways

Have you noticed God frequently doesn't do what seems logical to us? In Scripture, He often calls the most unlikely candidates and seems unconcerned with the cost or efficiency of His chosen methods.

Why waste billions of dollars to build a gold covered temple in Jerusalem? God doesn't live in a temple built by human hands. How can you justify such extravagance, especially when He knew the temple would be destroyed later? Shouldn't those funds have been used to "do justly" and help the poor? Judas asked the same question when a woman lavished expensive perfume upon the feet of Jesus.

By our standards God frequently doesn't seem to be a good steward of His resources. Jesus allowed Judas to remain as treasurer even though He certainly knew Judas was stealing. He never even confronted him about it. (John 12:6)

Saul was chastised for not destroying all the livestock of the Amalekites. But wasn't Saul simply being a "good steward," holding back the best to sacrifice to the Lord? He was doing what seemed logical, an act of good stewardship, instead of following God's directives? (1 Samuel 15)

The Lord has not revised or revoked His command to "Go into all the world." We dare not follow the example of Saul and try to improve on God's plan because it makes better financial sense to us. Money is not a problem for God – but disobedience is.

Obviously, I am not saying we are to be wasteful or squander His resources, but we must never forget they are *His* resources, not ours. I've heard people define "good stewardship" as wisely using the things the Lord has given us. That's close but not 100% accurate.

The Lord has not given them to us. A steward handles resources that belong to another. They remain His. We are simply entrusted to use them as He directs. Because they are His, we need to follow His directives on how they are spent, even if His plan does not seem the most wise, efficient or cost effective to us.

All Hands On Deck

Obedience is still God's measure for success, and the great commission command to "Go" is still in His Word. The task is so big we need "all hands on deck." We must continue to send foreign workers, national workers, and all who will respond to His call.

> While the harvest is white
> and the laborers few
> God sends national workers,
> foreign workers,
> perhaps even you.

Obedience is still God's measure of success.

He told them, "The harvest is plentiful, but the workers are few. Ask the Lord of the harvest, therefore, to send out workers into his harvest field.

- Luke 10:2

CHAPTER 3

STOP
"Sending Missionaries!"

To already "reached" nations.

I t was painful news. I wanted to give some words of encouragement but there was nothing helpful to say. A brokenhearted missionary couple had just told me their home church would no longer financially support their ministry because the Missions Board decided they were only going to support missionaries going to unreached people groups (UPGs).

What Is An Unreached People Group?

A UPG is a group of people with a common culture, language, or social class that do not have enough Christians in the group to evangelize the rest of the people without help from outside the group. A UPG will only be reached by sending outside reinforcements to aid the local Christians.

No one disputes the crucial need for sending missionaries to these people groups, but here are some problems I see with choosing to only support missionaries to UPGs.

It's About Discipleship

Certainly, we need to encourage more work among unreached people. But the command of Jesus was not just to reach people, not just to make converts. He said make disciples. That means reaching people is not enough. We can't just go; we must also stay. Making disciples is not as simple as:

> I preached, they prayed,
> all done, they're won.

Making disciples takes time. It means forming trusting relationships. It's not glamorous. It doesn't lend itself to measurable statistics or great photo ops. It certainly isn't as exciting as "going where no Christian has gone before," but it is what we are told to do.

It's About Obedience

I joined the military during wartime. I requested overseas duty but was assigned stateside. Surely the needs were greater over there–in the combat zone. But if I disregarded my orders and went to the front lines because I decided the need was greater there, I could have been court martialed for not being at my assigned post. Soldiers (and sailors like I was) must report for duty where they're assigned.

Missionaries are no different. They are to listen for their marching orders and go to their assigned post. To decide the need is greater somewhere else and launch out on their own is a dangerous game. Yes, there are fewer missionaries working with UPGs than in other areas of ministry, just like there are fewer soldiers on the front lines than scattered in bases and outposts around the globe. But each is fulfilling an essential role and worthy of our support.

It's About People

Some might ask, "If a church wants to support missionaries to UPGs couldn't their current missionaries simply relocate to where UPGs are?"

Sure they could but …

Missionaries and their families aren't inanimate pawns on a chess board that we can casually move from square to square whenever we get excited about a new strategy. Often, they have served for years, building trust and effective ministries in one area or among one group of people.

Learning the subtleties of a language, discovering keys to the culture and earning a hearing among a group of people can take decades. Moving means abandoning years of invested time, talent, and treasure and frankly, can mean going where they may feel no calling to serve.

Why The Double Standard?

Obviously, the US and Canada are reached countries. Should we no longer send missionaries to North American campuses? Should we no longer support missionaries working among the military or in urban slums, among the homeless and those enslaved in prostitution? Should we not support those fighting to stop the holocaust of abortion or human trafficking because the US and Canada are "reached" nations? We even support people to plant more churches in these church rich nations. And that's OK.

It's legitimate and necessary to support ministries that battle these crucial areas of darkness in our own "reached" nation. So, clearly, it's just as legitimate and necessary to support those who battle the same forces of darkness in other "reached" nations. Reaching is not enough. Teaching is not enough. The command is to make disciples.

Where Is Really "Reached"?

Should we stop supporting missionaries in the Philippines, Europe, Latin America, parts of Africa and Asia, or even North America because there are too many Christians in those countries?

Should missionaries abandon their work caring for orphans and widows, refugees and the outcast? Should they stop fighting human trafficking, salvaging discarded and abused women and children, caring for victims of war and violence, victims of disease, disintegrating family structures, and other fruits of sin and lost humanity, because the population has reached some randomly determined percentage of Christians?

Is There Not A Cause?

We need to send missionaries to UPGs, but there is still a need for those who, like Aaron and Hur, will come alongside strong national leaders to hold up their arms, encourage and serve. (Exodus 17) There are still astronomical needs in "reached" nations that require us to continue to send those God has called to those nations.

Trends come and go in missions, as they do in our secular society. But wisdom requires we not abandon all that has been done to this point to run after the latest fad. Instead, we must stay the course, follow the Lord's directions, and continue to "go and make disciples of **all** nations."

The command is not to just make converts. It is to make disciples of all nations.

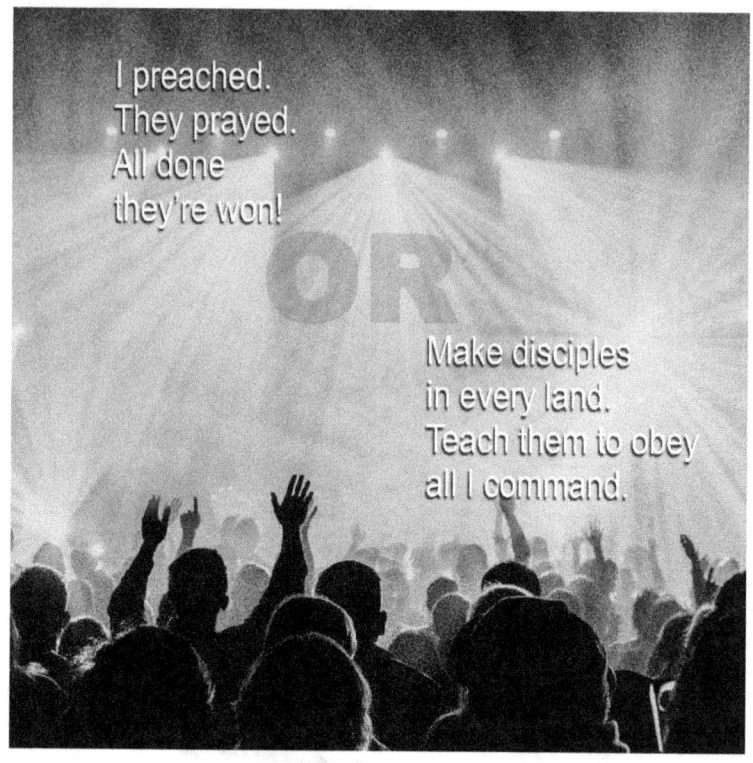

I preached.
They prayed.
All done
they're won!

OR

Make disciples
in every land.
Teach them to obey
all I command.

All authority in heaven and on earth has been given to me. Therefore, go and make disciples of all nations..."

- Matthew 28:18-19

CHAPTER 4

STOP
"Sending Missionaries!"

They destroy beautiful native cultures.

Repeat a lie often enough, and it will become a well-known fact. One such "fact" is that missionaries destroy local cultures. Obviously, missionaries make mistakes, and some have exported their own culture, thinking it was Biblical culture. But let me share a story that offers another perspective.

I had just finished working with a medical/dental team for two weeks in the mountain highlands of

Guatemala, Central America. On the way back to Guatemala City we stopped at one of the most gorgeous spots on Earth–Lake Atitlan. We crossed the lake by boat to visit some villages so the doctors could have a little break from the grueling schedule of the last two weeks.

A Picturesque Scene

I was walking with one of the doctors when we came across a woman, an indigenous Tzutujil Mayan, working under a tree beside the wide walking path we were following. A handmade fence of sticks, approximately 4 feet tall, separated us and outlined her family's small patch of dirt next to the trail. A one-room adobe home, complete with dirt floor, stood in one corner of the plot of land, and she sat in a corner close to the path. She was dressed in the colorful blouse and skirt of her tribe, though the colors were muted by dust and age. She sat in the dirt, weaving with a backstrap loom that is common in that area. We stopped for a moment to admire her artistry and the postcard scene.

The Truth Behind the Lovely Postcard

She was probably only in her forties, but a hard life gave her the appearance of a very weathered seventy-year-old. I told the doctor she would work on this piece for weeks or even months and then only make a few dollars for her labors. She probably had several children to care for and had likely lost one or two to disease, poor nutrition, or lack of prenatal care. If her husband was still with her, he might be hours away on the coast working in the cane fields, or he might be a drunkard who only comes home to rape her and take any money he can find. Village life is hard.

Tourist Meets Missionary

After a few moments a "turista" stopped and struck up a conversation. He said he was from Israel and asked what we were doing in Guatemala. The doctor answered, "I'm a medical missionary."

Our new friend responded, "I like the 'medical' part but I don't think I like the 'missionary' part. Missionaries destroy the native culture of the people."

My doctor friend calmly responded, "Just what part of their culture are you so concerned about preserving? Is it the part where a man routinely gets drunk and beats his wife? Or the part that treats women like beasts of burden? Or the part that forbids girls from getting an education that could help them escape their poverty? Or how about the part where most women cook over an open fire in a small room so their lungs are so full of smoke..."

Our new friend had turned and walked away. I think he was offended. But the doctor was being much kinder than I would have been.

They are People – Not Props!

After living, working and becoming friends with some of the Mayan people, the politically correct attitude of this tourist became reprehensible to me. It treats indigenous people as props in colorful photo ops, as animals in a living zoo that should be maintained "as is" for our viewing pleasure.

Those who promote the glorious virtues of the native cultures do not identify with the people enough to even see them as real human beings. What makes me say something so judgmental about their concerns for preserving the culture?

The Crucial Question

A simple question would let us know if it really is about preserving a valuable indigenous culture or more about not seeing the people as real human beings with real feelings, aspirations, hopes and dreams just like you and I have.

Here is the question: "If that was your mother sitting in the dirt, facing the hardships of daily life that this poor woman faces, would you be so committed to maintaining her culture or would you do something, whatever you could, to give her a better life?

"Could you snap a photo and walk away, muttering about how beautiful her life is, if that was your daughter and you knew there was a high probability of her being raped and pregnant by age 16? Would your primary concern be cultural preservation if it was your sister and you knew her lack of education and opportunity would result in her remaining trapped in poverty, sleeping in the dirt, with no access to medical or dental care and no hope of a brighter future?

"Would you encourage her to continue cooking in a tiny room over an open fire knowing that this quaint aspect of her culture produces over exposure to carbon dioxide producing respiratory illnesses and harming her children–both those already born and those in her womb?"

If I would not fight to preserve a culture that would subject my mother, daughter or sister to such misery, how can I think it's virtuous to insist someone else's mother, daughter or sister – or any human being – remain trapped in such wretchedness?

I wouldn't want to think it is simply because it makes for great photos. Or because it allows me to tell wonderfully interesting stories about how happy all these colorful people are. "See how they're smiling in my photos."

Mindless Excuses

Some have suggested, "They get used to it." Or "They don't know any better."

Really?

When you get close enough to these people that they open up and share their heart – their hopes, dreams and fears – you realize that's nonsense.

How does a person "get used" to the constant ache of hunger, or watching their children's hair thin and fall out because of malnutrition? Could you ever get used to watching your children die from easily curable diseases? If you are regularly beaten by your drunken husband or you are a teenage rape victim would it not bother you because you "don't know any better?" It's only detached "experts" who can pompously vomit such nonsense. (I told you my doctor friend was much kinder than I would have been.)

It's not that they don't know any better. It's not that they get used to it. It's not that they're committed to preserving the chains of their indigenous culture. It's that they have few options and the politically correct, zookeeper mentality – "Let's keep them poor and sitting in the dirt so we can take home amazing, colorful pictures to show our friends" - doesn't help them or their children.

What Changes Do You Oppose?

Yes, missionaries change cultures. In India, widows are no longer burned to death or expected to commit suicide because their husband died. Endless revenge killings and cannibalism are no longer the norm among many jungle tribes. I've actually heard supercilious scholars mourn the loss of even these horrendous aspects of "culture." Unbelievable!

Missionaries have fought to change indigenous cultures that practice female mutilation (wrongly called female circumcision), human sacrifice, and enslaving or slaughtering conquered tribes. They still fight today to save the lives and dignity of physically and mentally disabled children that are discarded as cursed by many cultures.

They seek to free people from alcoholism and drug addiction that tears apart families and the very fabric of society. They work to put an end to human trafficking, sex slavery, treating women like property and treating children like slaves required to work while being denied an education.

Do You Really Believe They Do It Alone?

But what thinking person believes a missionary can change a culture if the people don't see some personal benefit to the change? A missionary can't just say, "Do it this way," and have an entire group of people mindlessly obey. Like all of us, people change when they experience benefit to themselves and their family. Otherwise they don't.

Missionaries can't change cultures. Missionaries can only offer options. The people then decide what changes are of benefit to them and which ones aren't. Only the people themselves can change their culture.

Practice What You Preach

Finally, if you apply this "preserve the culture" philosophy to our own country, Thomas Edison, Henry Ford, Frederick Douglass, Harriet Tubman, and many others who changed the world for the better go from hero to villain. Our culture has certainly changed.

Unless you're Amish, you no longer depend on horses and buggies for transportation. Children no longer work sunup to sundown in coal mines or factories. Women can vote and no longer wash hand-made clothes with a scrub board. Slavery is illegal and education for children is mandatory.

For those who believe preserving native cultures is such a lofty goal, I suggest they try it at home before they sell it to others. Let them get rid of their cell phones, laptops and televisions that have so dramatically changed our culture. Let them go back to the roots of their culture and their ancestors' lifestyles.

Then, if they discover horses are better than cars, candles are better than electric lights, bloodletting beats penicillin, hunting is better than a supermarket, sleeping in dirt is better than their plush beds, etc., etc. Then they can authoritatively stand up and proclaim the glory of preserving native cultures.

Change Is Inevitable

With or without missionary involvement, cultures are going to change. Rather than destroying cultures, missionaries have often guided the change in positive ways that protected vulnerable populations from those who would exploit them.

Missionaries have been the ones who do the most to preserve the positive aspects of native cultures–often spending an entire lifetime learning a language, creating an alphabet, and then producing written records of rich tribal stories and traditions so the language and culture can be preserved.

When we see native people as real human beings with value equal to ours rather than props in a photo op, compassion will compel us to do all we can to help them improve their condition. But remember, people will only adopt cultural changes that prove beneficial to them.

41

They'll reject ones that aren't. Ultimately, it's up to them to preserve or change their culture.

Rather than destroying cultures, missionaries have often guided the inevitable change in ways that protected vulnerable populations from those who would exploit them.

HUMAN SACRIFICE · SATI burning a widow on her dead husband's funeral pyre · CHILD LABOR · CANNIBALISM · SPOUSAL ABUSE · KILLING "CURSED" (SPECIAL NEEDS) CHILDREN · FEMALE MUTILATION · ALCOHOLISM · SLAVERY · HUNGER · DRUG ADDICTION · DISEASE · TERROR / FEAR · FORCED ILLITERACY FOR WOMAN · ABJECT POVERTY · SUPERSTITION & EVIL SPIRITS · REVENGE KILLINGS

MISSIONARIES DESTROY BEAUTIFUL NATIVE CULTURES

DEVELOP A WRITTEN LANGUAGE TO PRESERVE THE HISTORY & CULTURAL STORIES · RESCUE ABANDONED CHILDREN · REDUCE INFANT MORTALITY · ESTABLISH MEDICAL CLINICS · ADVOCATE AGAINST THE VICTIMIZATION AND EXPLOITATION OF THE INDIGENOUS PEOPLE BY LAND SPECULATORS, OILMEN, CORPORATIONS, LUMBER COMPANIES, HUNTERS, GOVERNMENTS, ETC · DISASTER RELIEF WORK · IMPROVED FARMING METHODS TO REDUCE HUNGER AND STARVATION · TEACH BASIC HEALTH AND HYGIENE · TEACH LITERACY IN THE INDIGENOUS LANGUAGE AND NATIONAL LANGUAGE · VOCATIONAL TRAINING SO THE INDIGENOUS CAN SURVIVE WHEN THE OUTSIDE WORLD INEVITABLY INVADES THEIR LAND · FIGHT ABUSE AND EXPLOITATION OF WOMEN AND CHILDREN · FIGHT ALCOHOLISM, DRUG

I am sending you to them to open their eyes and turn them from darkness to light, and from the power of Satan to God, so that they may receive forgiveness of sins and a place among those who are sanctified by faith in me.'

- Acts 26:17-18

43

CHAPTER 5

STOP
"Sending Missionaries!"

That you would not hire to pastor your church.

The subject line on the email read, "Good article." I opened it to find a blog post by a missionary Bible translator from Africa. He was bemoaning the fact that "unqualified" people are sent as missionaries.

He then listed qualifications he would require of any missionary he supported. I laughed when I read some of them. But it was one of those broken hearted, "is this guy serious," kind of laughs. For example, he would not support a missionary who did not "teach the Bible chronologically."

Really? Obviously this guy had spent too many hours under the jungle sun without his pith helmet. I thought of some friends who work with street kids in Central America. Every day these kids beg or steal enough money to buy a small baggie from a street peddler. The baggie contains a bit of rubber cement. Inhaling the fumes dulls the pain of hunger and life in the street. But it also daily destroys more and more brain cells. Eventually they aren't even able to reason or function.

Teach the Bible chronologically? If my friends started in Genesis many of their street kid congregants would be dead long before they got to Leviticus. Maybe we can jump ahead to John 3:16 and work outward from there.

Why send those who are not theologically trained?

One missionary, who trains leaders in an African country, reports that, in his opinion, the leaders he works with "are frustrated with 'ordinary missionaries'". That, "above all, they want missionaries who are theologically trained.." And, of course, that would make sense. He works with leaders who are seeking to advance their own theological training. Naturally, they would hold an academic mindset and the limited perspective that goes with those who are seeking advanced theological training. But many, perhaps most, missionaries aren't sent to teach, train or help church leaders like these. They are sent to help those these church leaders are not reaching.

That's not to say these leaders are doing anything wrong. We need those who will fill pulpits and expound on the deep meaning of the Greek and Hebrew texts. We need those who can confront and debate the academic skeptics. But whether it's the United States or Uganda, Canada or Cambodia, there are hundreds of areas of darkness that are best addressed by those willing to step out from behind the academic teaching role of a pastor/teacher and go into the dark alleys and forgotten corners of our broken world.

If a missionary is going to train church leaders then go equipped with an understanding of hermeneutics, soteriology, pneumatology, ecclesiology, eschatology and all the other -ologies. But if you are called to reach into the pit and rescue those enslaved in deep darkness then perhaps the same training and equipping that the "unlearned and ignorant" Peter and John demonstrated is adequate - boldness and having spent time with Jesus. (Acts 4:13)

Why Send Someone You Would Not Hire?

Another blogger, with what seemed like reasonable logic, asked, "Why would you send someone that you would never hire as a pastor in your own church?" At first glance that makes good sense, except the skills necessary for a successful overseas ministry and those needed for a North American based pastor are often totally different. Most missionaries do not pastor. In many places being a "pastor" is one of the least effective ways to reach people.

Pastors fill pulpits and spend their time hanging around church buildings. If the lost routinely dropped into churches that might be an effective way to reach them. But, most missionaries are in the fields, tracking down the lost ones, not in the sheepfold caring for the 99.

Both are valid and needed ministries but rescuing lost sheep and caring for those in the fold are dramatically different callings. It's like comparing a pioneer to a settler, a hunter-gatherer to a farmer, a John the Baptist to a Timothy. John was a great front-line evangelist but I doubt that his people skills would lend to successful pastoring.

Caring for children in an orphanage, teaching world history in a school for missionary kids, rescuing women from sex trafficking and teaching them a trade, plus thousands of other ministries don't require extensive theological training but are effective ways to fulfill the great commission. So, yes, it makes sense to send into the harvest field those you would not hire to stay home and tend the sheep. God still uses "unschooled, ordinary men" who have "been with Jesus." (Acts 4:13)

The first missionary we sent through Commission To Every Nation went into a mountain village in the highlands of Guatemala. He was barely a high school graduate. He had attended a good Bible teaching church but was certainly no theologian. He served as an agriculture missionary, helped where he could and built solid relationships with the people. One day a knock came on his door. The pastor of a local church had a request. "Will you teach me the Bible?"

They started studying the book of Romans. This loved, respected but barely literate local pastor had led the church for over ten years but had had no opportunity for any form of training. His first question, "Who wrote the book of Romans?" My unschooled, untrained friend, who would never be called to pastor a church in the US, was able to offer invaluable insight and help this respected local pastor grow in his understanding of the Lord and His Word. In addition, though this missionary was not a college graduate, he found himself leading teams of college students. Though he had no medical training, he found himself as an essential member of medical teams, leading, translating and serving wherever needed.

There are many places where love and an open heart will do more to preach the gospel than multiple seminary degrees. It is astounding what God will do when we make ourselves available to be used by Him. But let's hear from another untrained, unskilled missionary.

Gladys Aylward was a British missionary to China before and during World War II. The film, *The Inn of the Sixth Happiness*, is based on her work but presents a highly fictionalized account. The book, *The Small Woman*, by Alan Burgess, presents a more accurate picture of her life and ministry.

A Bit of Background

Gladys was from a working-class family in London. Her only job skill was as a maid. Feeling called to China she began studying Chinese but the mission agency dismissed her because she was not making adequate progress. Spending her life savings, she bought a ticket to China on the Trans-Siberian Railway. It was a perilous trip and she only managed to survive and eventually arrive in China because of many miraculous Divine interventions.

Finally, in China, she worked with an older missionary running an inn, caring for orphans, working with prisoners and risking her life multiple times doing "foolish" things to help the poor and disenfranchised masses.

In 1938, Japan brutally invaded China and Gladys led over 100 orphans on a treacherous journey to safety. When the Communists took control of China they went on a "search and destroy mission" to eliminate missionaries. Only then did she return to Britain where she cared for her elderly mother. Upon the death of her mother she tried to return to China but was denied a visa. In 1958, she settled in Taiwan and began the Gladys Aylward Orphanage where she served until her death in 1970 at the age of 67. She is not one you would hire to pastor a church in the US or England but God used this "handmaiden" of the Lord to do amazing things in China.

This transcript comes from a recording sometime after her return to Britain in 1948. In her own words, she talks about her training, qualifications and preparation for such a spectacular missionary career.

Her Training and Preparation

"When I went to China I had never seen a Chinese person. I didn't even know where China was. To me it was just a black dot on the map somewhere. And I'm afraid I had a terrific shock when I got there to find how large it was. I only knew that little, green island of England, and now before me stretched that great, huge, wonderful and beautiful land with its teeming millions of aching and hungry hearts. I truly believe He asked me to go.

"You see one day He walked along and crossed my path and He said 'come,' and I went. And He said, 'You can't do anything, you know. I'll do it through you.'

"And I remember going home when I felt God was calling me to China and saying to my father, 'You know dad, I would like to go to China.' And my father, rather a silent sort of man, but pretty straight, and he sat there and said, 'And what do you think you are going to do?'

"And I said, 'I don't know.'

"Well you're not a nurse are you?'

'No, no I'm not.'

"Well you can't nurse anybody.'

'No,' I said, 'no I can't.'

'And you can't teach anything can you?'

'No,' I said, 'I can't.'

"And then he suddenly swung around and looked at me and said, 'O God, get out,' he said, 'All you can do is talk.'

"And I remember turning back and going outside the kitchen door and standing in that little passage at the bottom of the stairs and having and... well... having a little weep. He didn't understand, bless him, because, you see, God hadn't called him. He had called me.

"And then, suddenly, in the middle of my tears. There came this: Well, isn't that it?

"And so, standing there I said, 'O Lord, well, he said talk. Well, all right then, I'll talk. And I'll talk and I'll talk and I'll talk and I'll talk and I'll just keep on talking but it will be for you.'

"Nobody, least of all my dear father, dreamed of how true his words were going to become. Almost from that very moment God put words into my mouth and I've talked solidly ever since."

Study, Strategy and Skill – No Guarantee of Success

While there's no reason to applaud or imitate Gladys' ignorance of the country and culture, especially with so much information easily accessible to us today, it demonstrates that effectiveness is not dependent upon study, strategies, or skills. Availability is still the most important ability God looks for in those He uses.

That's not to say God is opposed to training and skills. There's no virtue in ignorance. Repeatedly the Bible tells us to "get wisdom," to study to show ourselves approved. Ecclesiastes compares education to sharpening an axe. It's easier to cut down a tree with a sharp axe than with a dull one. (Ecclesiastes 10:10)

The two men who wrote the majority of the New Testament—Paul and Luke—were both highly educated. But highly educated Paul had to lay aside "lofty words and impressive wisdom." He had to reduce his message to nothing but "Jesus Christ and him crucified." (1 Corinthians 2:1-2) While uneducated Peter tells us we shouldn't stay ignorant - "make every effort to add to your faith goodness; and to goodness, knowledge." (2 Peter 1:5 NIV)

Training, education and experience are all very positive ways to "sharpen your axe" but with all of that, be sure the most important lessons you are learning are humility and a dependence upon the Lord because, apart from Him we can do nothing. (John 15:5)

The Key To Being Used By God

We shouldn't think God can't use us because we lack education, but we should also take advantage of every opportunity to learn and "sharpen the axe." The key here is humility. If we're proud of our education or proud of our ignorance, God Himself will stand against our efforts. He resists the proud but gives grace to the humble. (James 4:6, 1 Peter 5:5)

I am convinced that God is most glorified when He uses the least qualified because then there can be no question as to who deserves the credit. Why else would He choose a trembling Gideon, a lustful Samson, shepherds to testify of His birth and a group of fishermen to tell of His death. Why else would He use you and me?

God is most glorified
when He uses the least qualified.

Father,

I feel so inadequate

And I'm glad I do.

Cause Lord,

if I were adquate,

I'd have no need of

You.

This is what the Lord says:
"Let not the wise boast of their wisdom
or the strong boast of their strength
or the rich boast of their riches,
but let the one who boasts boast about this:
that they have the understanding to know me,
that I am the Lord, who exercises kindness,
justice and righteousness on earth,
for in these I delight," declares the Lord.

Jeremiah 9:23-24

CHAPTER 6

STOP
"Sending Missionaries!"

Who don't do "real" missionary work.

P
ith helmets and machetes. Cannibals and jungle huts. Dugout canoes cutting a path through piranha infested waters. What images flood your imagination when you hear the term "missionary?"

You probably don't envision an upscale urban coffee shop or a surfer hanging out at the beach. How about a street actor or a North American teacher, sharpening his pencil to prepare to teach English to a class of American kids. But all of those are actual overseas, foreign missionary activities. In fact, there is a place in missions for anyone who has a desire to serve.

But what is "real" missions work and are those people "real" missionaries?

A "Real" Missionary Answers

One missionary church planter didn't think so. She tells how she and her husband were "real missionaries." In fact, she confessed, "we looked down on those who had support roles." Yes, there were accountants and tech people who helped keep things running but the "real missionaries" were the church planters. In her mind, all these other people were just taking up resources that could be funneled into doing real missions work.

But, then something amazing happened. She had a child. As kids tend to do, the child grew older and eventually needed an education. The national schools were substandard and would not have prepared their daughter with the necessary skills and education. She could homeschool but that would take Mom away from doing "real" missions ministry. Plus, she didn't see homeschooling as a viable option for her.

Suddenly the ministry of those "not real missionaries" became very real. She saw how essential these teachers were in enabling translators, church planters, pastors and missionary Bible teachers to fulfill their call. Suddenly she was crying desperately for more, not fewer, of these support role, real missionaries.

Statistics vary as to how many support people it takes to keep one front line soldier in the battle. But, when the US engaged in World War II it took the entire nation to win the war. Some contributed by working in factories. Some grew "victory gardens," cut back on their consumption of items needed for the war effort and purchased war bonds. By producing planes and munitions, sewing uniforms and writing letters, driving truckloads of food and gasoline, recruiting and reporting on the progress, everyone did what they could.

There was something for everyone to do. Kids even sacrificed a shiny new bike for Christmas (perhaps not always voluntarily) as the government suspended production of kid's bicycles so precious rubber and metal could be directed toward the war effort. The paymaster accountant was as crucial as the pilot. The mechanic as necessary as the frontline foot soldier. The plumber and the sharpshooter all had a critical role to play. World-wide Missions is much the same way. There is a place for every skill, every talent and everybody.

But coffee shops and surfing? Get Real!

But what about that upscale urban coffee shop?

You mean the one in a post-modern capital city in Europe, where young men and women who would never attend a traditional church will come and open up with the owners about their fears, doubts and futures?

And the surfer hanging out on the beach?

You must be referring to the one in a world-famous surf town known for its bars and brothels because of the regular flow of foreigners seeking "the Endless Summer." You could open a church there – and she does work with a local church - and hope some of these traveling vagrants accidentally stumble in. But her presence in their world – much like Jesus came to our world – reaches out to them in a culturally relevant way.

And the street actor?

The one that, with a team of performers, does impromptu street theater in Muslim countries and boldly proclaims the gospel, handing out gospel literature and talking with anyone who expresses interest in hearing more about Isa (Jesus).

"Real missionaries" are just real people in love with a real Jesus who have offered their real gifts, talents, skills and passions as real tools to reach a desperately lost world in search of real answers.

Some of us are called to the front lines. Some of us are called to support. But all of us are invited into the exciting mission – the Great Co-Mission – of partnering with the Lord Jesus Christ to take His love and redemption to the ends of the earth – every tribe, every nation, every tongue, every culture.

Are you doing something real with your life? Each of us has something to give, some way we can be part of the great adventure the Lord invites us into. What are you doing with your Labor, Influence, Finances and Expertise – Your **L.I.F.E**?

Labor

One of the greatest needs on the mission field is people who are simply willing to work hard. One fellow asked me, "I'm not very smart but I can work hard. Is there a place for me in missions?" And, of course, there was a place for him – lots of places actually. He later went to serve as a missionary with Commission To Every Nation. In fact, I thought, that might be a pretty good job description for a missionary – "Looking for people who are not very smart but can work hard." After all, what "smart" person leaves home and family, career and country, to raise their own support and go serve people they don't even know and who, sometimes, don't even appreciate them being there?

Some years ago, I was contacted by the board of a mission that fed and clothed the poor. They needed help and asked if I knew of anyone who might be interested. I chuckled when they told me the primary qualification.

"We don't need a preacher or teacher. We already have too many of those. We need someone who can do something."

Can you do something? Are you willing to roll up your sleeves and get your hands dirty for God? If so, there is a place where you can do it and make an eternal difference.

Influence

John Maxwell said, "Everyone is a leader because everyone influences someone." We live in an age where influence is not limited to a few celebrities or famous people. Thanks to social media we all have a platform from which we can influence countless people – many of whom we may never meet in person. By doing something as easy as sharing or creating a post about a missionary or ministry we can spread the word and let others know of opportunities.

By using your influence and introducing those in your sphere of influence – family, friends, neighbors, co-workers and others - to missions and missionaries, you

65

can become a crucial link to help the work of the Lord go forward.

Finances

A friend was coming to join our ministry in Guatemala but his first question was, "Is it possible for me to get a job there rather than raise my support?" With his talents, my friend probably could have gotten a job but, I explained to him, that if he did get a job he wouldn't have time to be of help to the missionaries that desperately needed his skills and full-time service. To be effective he would need to raise support.

Most missionaries must look to friends, family and churches to fund their work. And that is perhaps the biggest stumbling block for many potential missionaries. It's hard to ask people for money even for a vital and eternal cause that you believe in and are willing to give your life to. There is concern that you might be misunderstood or that it might damage a friendship. Let's face it, money is a sensitive issue and our independent culture frowns upon looking to others for help.

But, when a missionary seeks support so they can minister full-time they are following the example of Paul. He was only able to minister one day a week when he was tentmaking. But after Silas and Timothy arrived he was able to minister the word full time. Can you figure out why? (Acts 18:1-5)

While support raising can seem to be a huge stumbling block for an aspiring missionary, I believe it is one of the sweetest parts about God's plan of sending missionaries. It enables everyone to participate and share in the work of world evangelism. Those who, for whatever reason, can't go themselves can help others go and share in the excitement and reward. (Matthew 10:41-42)

Did you know that Jesus had people who supported Him financially? He could feed thousands with a little bread and two fish. He could have tossed a rock to Peter and have it turn into a loaf of bread before Peter caught it. He didn't need people to give to Him. I would have expected Him to suggest they give their gifts to the poor instead of to Him. But he received their gifts as a way for them to participate in His ministry and, He so valued their partnership, that He even made sure their names were recorded in the eternal Scriptures. (Luke 8:3)

The command, and joyous opportunity, to tell the nations about the God of love and forgiveness is shared with all of us. (2 Corinthians 5:17-21) You can be a vital part of a missionary's ministry, enabling them to give full attention to the ministry because of your investment – and, when you do, you will receive the same reward they do for their work. (Matthew 10:41-42)

Expertise

He wasn't a preacher, teacher or Bible scholar but he was one of our favorite part-time missionaries. He was a mechanic who owned a shop in Florida. Once a year he closed his shop for two weeks, brought tools and his technicians to the mission field to do what they did best - repair cars. It was an amazing gift from a man using his expertise to advance the gospel.

Roads in many countries chew up cars like meat through a grinder. I had parts replaced that I didn't even know existed – because they never wear out on smooth US roads. We always had a full schedule of repairs for vehicles that transported translators, church planters, kids from children's homes, food and supplies to remote villages. This mechanic and his team had an immeasurable impact upon the safety and security of missionaries and missions work simply by using their area of expertise to bless the nations.

Accountant or architect, farmer or fence builder, lawyer, librarian, veterinarian, videographer, X-ray tech or zoologist – literally A-Z, whatever your skill, there is a place for you to use your expertise on the mission field.

What are you doing with your L.I.F.E. to make an eternal difference?

Then I heard the voice of the Lord saying, "Whom shall I send? And who will go for us?" And I said, "Here am I. Send me!"

- Isaiah 6:8

CONCLUSION

STOP
Sending Missionaries!

Go with them.

S ome years ago a number of churches collaborated
on an advertising campaign that featured this
surprising phrase:

Stop sending your kids to church!

What!?

Churches encouraging parents to not send their kids to
church?

That initial statement was followed up with two words:

Take them.

In the same way, I suggest we should stop sending missionaries if sending implies waving goodbye, wishing them well and then getting on with our lives – out of sight, out of mind.

Obviously, we don't need to "take them" to their assigned field but there are important ways we can go with them.

Of course, you can "go with them" through praying for them - getting updates from them so you are aware of what is happening in their lives and how to pray specifically for them.

But, more important than praying for them, I suggest you invest in their ministry. Invest? Yes, by sending real money to them on a regular basis.

As I've already mentioned, most missionaries depend upon friends and family members to support their ministry financially so they can do what they do.

Without a team of financial backers – just like Jesus had (Luke 8:3) - they aren't able to serve.

After all, most countries don't want foreigners coming in and taking jobs from their people and, if the missionary does work a secular job, it often means he or she has little time to devote to ministry because of all the extra complications associated with living outside their home country.

Isn't prayer more important than money?

Before I ever thought about serving as a missionary my pastor told me how impressed he was with a missionary who told his congregation, "Don't give to me if you aren't going to pray for me. I don't want to go if I don't have people praying for me."

When I became a missionary and was actively raising support to go I remembered that story. Can I be honest with you? I thought, "Forget that! That sounds real spiritual but if you are deciding between praying and giving, I'd rather you give. I can pray for myself." Plus, my wife has an amazing prayer connection with the

Lord. If she is praying about something you might as well get ready because it's going to happen.

I know it sounds pretty unspiritual to say you prefer folks giving over them praying but it actually is in line with Biblical principles. Prayers for missionaries are important. Nothing of eternal importance happens without God's involvement. But, Jesus said that where your treasure is, your heart will follow. (Matthew 6:21)

In other words, when you invest your hard-earned money into a missionary your heart will be there, too. That means your prayer will be more passionate, more effective and more long-lasting. If you simply commit to pray for a missionary, for most of us that means, at best, a one-and-done quick prayer. Forget it and move on.

But when you are investing monthly you are investing a part of yourself. You become a part – a partner – in that ministry and your heart follows. If you are giving, investing regularly in the work I am doing, then I know you are also regularly thinking about and praying for me.

If I give $1000 to a missionary in Thailand, every time Thailand is mentioned in even a brief newscast it will catch my attention. "What happened?! What's going on in Thailand? Part of my heart is there." I have invested "treasure" there and where my treasure is my heart is too.

But I have so little I can give

It's easy to think my little gift won't make a difference. But how big does a seed have to be before it is worth planting? Remember Jesus' illustration of the tiny mustard seed that could grow into a large tree but ... only if it was planted. And the story about Jesus commending the widow who gave next to nothing but it was all she had. (Mark 12:43) One dear saint planted $3.00 a month into our ministry for years before her home-going. We treasured that sacred gift each month and, I'm convinced, the Lord did, too.

We all have something we can give. The size of the seed does not matter as long as we plant it. The size of the heart behind the gift is what the Lord examines.

Help God Fulfill a Promise to a Friend

By giving to missions - taking the gospel around the world - we are part of what God is doing to fulfill a promise he made to a friend of his – Abraham.

God promised that Abraham would be a blessing to all nations. That was a prophetic word referring to the coming of Jesus. Jesus has come but not all nations know it. For them to believe and be blessed, for the promise to be fulfilled, they must first hear. That means someone must go tell them. That means someone must be sent.

How then can they call on the One in whom they have not believed? And how can they believe in the One of whom they have not heard? And how can they hear without someone to preach? And how can they preach unless they are sent? (Romans 10:14-15)

So, what's keeping you from stepping into the exciting arena of world missions? You can give. Then you can pray. And, yes, you can even go. Long-term or short-term, there is a place for you in taking the gospel to the nations. You can be part of helping the Lord fulfill a promise made 4000 years ago to a dear friend. Now **that** is a God who is serious about keeping His promises.

> **John Piper** ✔ @JohnPiper · Mar 3
> You have three choices in world missions: be a joyful, sacrificial goer, be a joyful, sacrificial sender, or be disobedient.

For help in finding your place and taking the first step into missions, contact Commission To Every Nation (www.cten.org) or Commission Ministers Network. (www.CMNetwork.org)

Browse the websites. You'll find many hardworking missionaries and national workers you can partner with by giving, praying, going for a visit or to work alongside them long-term or short-term.

STOP sending missionaries?

The day will come - at "the end of the age"- when it's time to STOP. But until then we must obey the command to GO.

*"I have been given all authority
in heaven and on earth.*

*Therefore, go and make disciples
of all the nations,
baptizing them in the name of the Father
and the Son and the Holy Spirit.*

*Teach these new disciples
to obey all the commands
I have given you.
And be sure of this:
I am with you always,
even to the end of the age."*

-- Jesus --

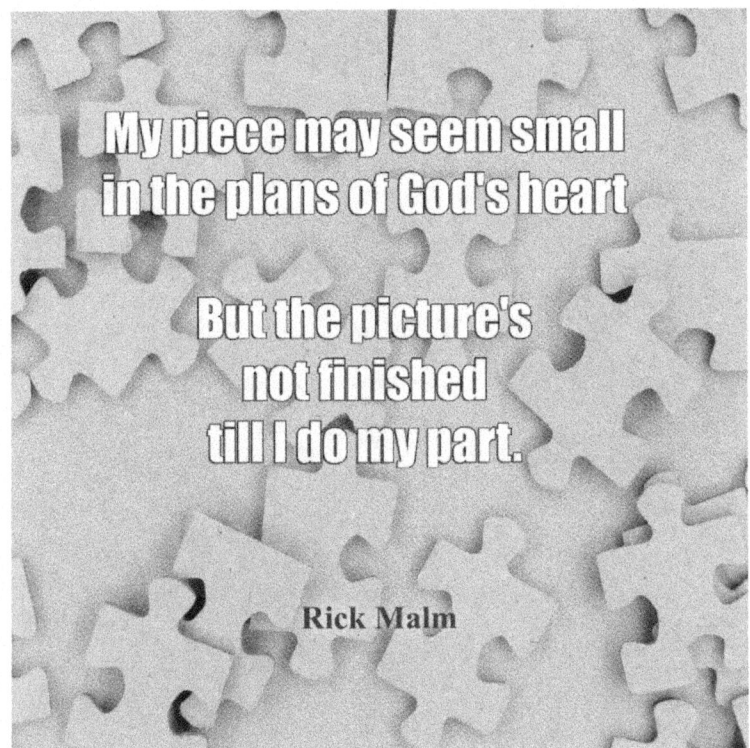

Notes, Thoughts and Steps of Action

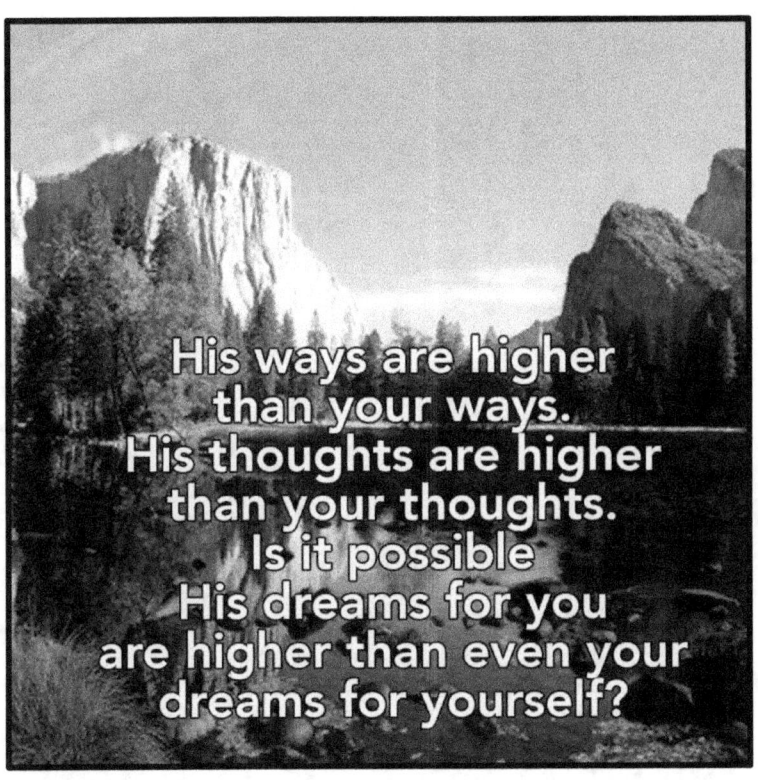

His ways are higher
than your ways.
His thoughts are higher
than your thoughts.
Is it possible
His dreams for you
are higher than even your
dreams for yourself?

ABOUT THE AUTHOR

Richard Malm is founder of
Commission To Every
Nation and Commission
Ministers Network. These
two organizations have sent
over 1000 missionaries
and national workers
into over 85 nations.

He is a pastor, missionary, Christian educator,
parent, grandparent and husband to Jana for over 45
years.

He holds a BA in Business Management, an MS in
Educational Administration and, in the unlikely
event that he decides to complete his doctoral thesis,
he will earn a PhD in Pastoral Ministry.

He resides in the Hill Country of Texas where he
enjoys feeding the birds, the pesky deer and spending
time with his amazing wife, kids and grandchildren.

You can connect with him at www.RickMalm.com

MORE FROM RICK

Commission To Every Nation

How People Just Like You Are Blessing the Nations

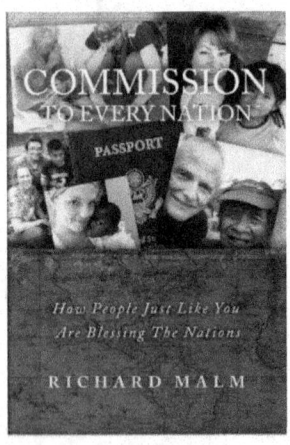

Have you ever felt unqualified to do something for God?

You're not alone. Rick Malm's pastor actually told him, "You're the most unlikely candidate for ministry I've ever met." Ouch!

But when Rick and his family moved to war-torn Guatemala, God engineered a thrilling, atypical path to founding an agency that has sent thousands of Christians around the world.

Commission To Every Nation is more than just the story of one man's reluctant journey to begin an international missions agency. It's the story of how God uses ordinary people to accomplish extraordinary results for His glory.

What others are saying:

- A great read that had me laughing out loud one minute, wiping tears the next.

- Funny, insightful, thought provoking but, most of all, relateable. Get a copy STAT.

- We're reading CTEN in our fellowship group. Really good!

- I devoured it! It stirred up my vision for what I always believed God wanted me to do.

- I couldn't put it down. I finished it in one sitting.

- A must read, especially for those of us who have felt horribly unqualified to ever be used by God.

- One of the best books on missions I have read in 50 years of ministry.

- I've never read a book that had such a direct impact on my life.

- It so grabbed my attention that I ended up finishing it in just a few hours - and marked it all up.

- I could't put it down! Loved it!

- I got up at 3am to finish it.

Five Reasons I'm Grateful
I Raise Support

The very thought of it strikes fear into the heart of even the bravest missionary. "I'll swim with piranha, eat monkey brains and confront malaria but please don't make me ... raise support!"

"Grateful" is a book for both support raisers and donors. "Grateful" will encourage and inspire you to gratitude for the privilege of being part of the support raising adventure.

Spare the Rod
Five Times You Should Not Spank Your Child

Introductory principles on parenting.

Isn't spanking a barbaric form of discipline that has no place in modern society?

Doesn't spanking a child teach them that violence is an appropriate way to solve problems?

Or, is it possible that when done within Biblical guidelines spanking is not an act of violence but is actually a controlled act of love that helps a child escape slavery to his or her own selfishness, unrestrained emotions and unbridled will?

Much more than just a book about spanking children.

Spare the Rod provides guidelines that apply to all aspects of training children. It examines when it is appropriate to use corporal punishment, when it is not and the proper heart attitude a parent should have when exercising any form of reprimand or child discipline.

I Like Flowers

A fun book for parent and child. Rick wrote *I Like Flowers* to share with his grandchildren. Now you and your child can enjoy this colorful, visual treat filled with images of flowers taken by Rick on his travels to over 50 nations.

You and your child will enjoy exploring again and again the vibrantly colored flowers and leaves, cactus and trees while carried along on fun verse, simple rhyme and twists of humor.

Order at: www.RickMalm.com/books